THE ROYAL FEAST

DAVY LIU

For the Sovereign One

Grateful acknowledgement
to Laura Derico for her creative input and insight.

The Royal Feast
ISBN: 9781937212292
Updated Edition - First Printing: July 2016
Published by Green Egg Media, Inc.
Irvine, California
greeneggmediagroup.com

Text and Illustrations copyright 2010 and 2016 by
Kendu Films, LLC. California
kendufilms.com

Printed in Korea through Codra Enterprises, Inc.
codra.com

The sun was hot as the father porcupine called to his children. "Quills out!"
"Like this?" Spike asked.

Spike's friend Belzar, a young lion, was amazed at the long, sharp quills.

"Perfect!" said the father. "That will keep you safe from our enemies, the Zebs!"

Belzar wanted quills too. "I don't even have a mane," he said.

Spike jumped on top of his friend's head, "Here you go!"

The two friends laughed. "Now I look like a real lion!"

"No, you look like a real porcupine!" Spike giggled.

Belzar was happy to be part of the porcupine family. They had taken care of him since he was a tiny cub. But he always wondered what had happened to his lion family.

Suddenly, they heard the sound of hooves.
It was the Zebs!

"So what are you?" the leader of the gang snorted.
"A porcu-lion?"

"Well, he can't be a real lion!" another Zeb teased.
"He couldn't even catch a turtle!"

Belzar stood tall. "I could catch you if I wanted to!"

"Prove it!" the leader challenged. "Let's race to the top
of that hill. Ready . . . set . . . go!"

Belzar took off as fast as he could. But he was not fast enough.

The Zebs laughed at Belzar.

But then the leader said, "You have one more chance.
Prove you are a real lion. Jump up and grab the meat
hanging from that branch!"

Spike's quills were tingling. He knew it was a trick!
"Belzar, don't—"

But Belzar had already sprung into the air.

A deep hole was dug under the branch.
Belzar fell down, down into the trap.

The Zebs sneered down into the pit.

"Aww, poor lion. You look just like your parents did
when we tricked them!" And they laughed and laughed.

The sound of wheels made the Zebs run.
The ones the animals called "two-feeters" came and
pulled Belzar out of the pit they had made.

As they carted him away, Belzar heard Spike's voice.
"I will get you out, Belzar! I promise!"

The cart entered a big city at sunset. Torches lit the way.

Suddenly, one of those torches fell. The cart was on fire!

The horse pulling the cart reared up, and the cage
fell over. Belzar was afraid! "Help!"

A two-feeter dressed in rich robes appeared and
pulled the young lion out.

Belzar was so tired and scared, he looked into the man's
face and fainted in his arms.

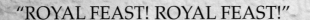

"ROYAL FEAST! ROYAL FEAST!"

Belzar awoke to the sound of growling.

He blinked his eyes as he looked around.
Many pairs of eyes stared back at him.

Belzar saw that he was in a huge underground cave.
A cave filled with lions!

A big lion came up to him. "I am King Nebu.
And you are not my feast! Who are you?"

"I'm Belzar. Where am I?"

King Nebu laughed. "Come. Let me show you my palace."
As they walked, Belzar told King Nebu about the river
lands, his porcupine family, and about the mean Zebs.

King Nebu told Belzar about life in his palace.
He told Belzar that, on special days, a royal feast
dropped from above. All the lions ate as much
as they liked.

"Life in my palace is safe and easy," King Nebu said.

"That sounds good," Belzar said. "But I need to go
back to the river lands. I need to show those Zebs that
I'm a real lion."

Belzar looked at King Nebu's flowing mane.

"Would you teach me how to grow a mane?
Then I will be powerful—like a real lion!"

"Belzar, a mane does not give power. A lion's true power comes from knowing what is right and good. Learn that first. The mane will come."

King Nebu taught Belzar many more things. Belzar told him many stories of the river lands. As time passed, the two became very close, like father and son.

But King Nebu's own son, Zuma, was jealous. He did not like Belzar's stories. Zuma became angry with Belzar, and his father too.

The palace had many tunnels that the lions never entered. All the lions stayed close to where the royal feast was dropped.

But Zuma needed a trap. And he found it.

Zuma said, "Father, I heard a strange sound!
You are so brave, and Belzar likes to explore.
Can you two come listen in this tunnel?"

In the tunnel, Belzar and King Nebu could not see the dark pit in front of them. But Zuma knew it was there.

Suddenly, the king and Belzar were tumbling down into darkness.

"It is time for a new leader," Zuma roared.
"One who does not listen to silly stories!"

Once again, Belzar was in a dark pit. But this time
he was not alone.

Belzar watched King Nebu lick the cuts he had
from falling against the sharp rocks. At first he was sad.
Then Belzar became angry.

"Zuma is a bully, just like those Zebs! I want to go back
to the river lands and to my family! ROAR!!!"

Belzar had never roared so loud. The sound shook
the cave. Part of the wall crumbled.

Suddenly, rays of light broke through the darkness.
A shadowy figure appeared.

"Spike!" Belzar's eyes were wide with surprise.

Spike grinned. "I told you I would get you out! A bird
helped me find the palace where the cart took you.
I used my nose to smell my way to the lions.
Then I smelled the way to you!"

King Nebu was happy to meet the porcupine
that Belzar had told him so much about.

"Let's get out of here!" Spike said.

The friendly bird and Spike led the way back
to the river lands.

King Nebu was amazed at the open spaces. All he had ever known were the shadowy rooms of the palace.

Belzar and King Nebu hunted and played together. Spike was happy to have his friend and brother back.

But it was not long before the Zebs returned.
One day they snuck up behind Spike. They did not
see Belzar and King Nebu in the reeds close by.

"Well, Spiky, are you back from your lion hunt?
Where is your friend?" the leader teased. "Did the
two-feeters eat him?"

Suddenly Belzar roared! He and King Nebu leaped
toward the Zebs. The bullies saw Belzar and screamed
in terror. They galloped away as fast as their legs
would go!

Spike could not stop laughing. "Did you see their faces?
They will never come back here again!"

King Nebu was proud. "Belzar, you did it!
You proved to those Zebs that you are a real lion.
Now it is time for me to show my son and all the others
how to be real lions too. I must go back to my palace."

Belzar did not want to leave the river lands. But he said,
"I am a true lion. And I know what is right, King Nebu.
I will go with you."

"I will go with you too, brother," Spike said.

Back at the palace, the lions missed King Nebu.

Zuma was a bad king.

He did not know what was right and good.

He did not care for the other lions. He kept the best part of the feasts for himself, and gave the others only scraps.

With Spike's help, King Nebu and Belzar found their
way back to the palace.

King Nebu heard the whines of the hungry lions.
Then he saw Zuma eating the last of the feast.
He let out an angry "ROAR!"

The lions were so happy to see their true king.
But Zuma was not happy at all. He leaped from the
feast table and charged toward his father.

Seconds before his teeth could reach King Nebu's neck,
Spike jumped into his path.

"Take that!" Spike shouted.

"OUCH!!!" Zuma cried out in pain as the quills jabbed
into his face.

The lions gathered around to greet Belzar and King Nebu, and to meet their new friend, Spike.

"How did you get out, King Nebu? Where have you been?" they asked.

King Nebu told them about the river lands.

"River lands?" snorted Zuma, as he pulled quills out of his face. "The palace is where lions belong."

"No, my son," King Nebu said. "Real lions were made to roam in the river lands, where life is not safe and easy. True life is not about waiting for a royal feast. It is about waking up every day to a new adventure."

Just then somewhere overhead a stone was rolled away. Light shone down into the cave. The lions began chanting again, "ROYAL FEAST! ROYAL FEAST!"

King Nebu led Belzar to the feast table. "Belzar, you are a real lion now. Eat your royal feast. Then let's return to the river lands."

Belzar looked up. He saw rich robes. He saw a dark mane. He saw a familiar face. It was the two-feeter who saved him when his cage was on fire!

Belzar turned away from the table. "I know what is right and good, and I cannot eat this feast. This two-feeter saved me from danger. Now I must save him."

Belzar stood tall. "If any of you wants to eat him, you will have to eat me first."

The hungry lions licked their lips and stared at the table.

As they stared, a bright light filled the palace. King Nebu bowed before the feast, then sat down beside Belzar, with his mouth shut tight.

One by one, the lions all sat, with their mouths shut firmly—even Zuma.

That night, all the lions went to sleep hungry.
And in the morning, the royal feast vanished.

Zuma woke King Nebu. "Father, I know what is right
now. And I have been doing wrong. Will you forgive
me?"

King Nebu rose and smiled at his son. "Yes, Zuma.
Now let's go and live like real lions!"

King Nebu, Belzar, and Spike led all the lions out of the
palace and to the river lands. There the lions learned to
hunt and run. They lived the way lions were made to
live. And they found new adventures every day.

Artist and Author Davy Liu immigrated to the United States at age 13. Within a few months, his talent for drawing and painting was discovered.

At age 19 Davy began a career in feature films working for Disney Studios, Warner Bros and Industrial Light and Magic. His work has appeared in *The Beauty and The Beast, Aladdin, Mulan, The Lion King* and *Star Wars Episode I.*

Every year Davy speaks to over 250,000 people, sharing his inspirational story of overcoming the incredible odds he faced in his youth.

To learn how to draw characters from the Invisible Tails series and to see Davy's speaking schedule, go to InvisibleTails.com